Trevor's Trousers

by

David Webb

First Published
January 05 in Great Britain by

PUBLISHING

ISBN-10: 1-904904-19-X
ISBN-13: 978-1-904904-19-X

Educational Printing Services Limited
Albion Mill, Water Street, Great Harwood, Blackburn BB6 7QR
Telephone: (01254) 882080   Fax: (01254) 882010
E-mail: enquiries@eprint.co.uk   Website: www.eprint.co.uk

Contents

Chapter 1
A New Pair of Trousers

Trevor's trousers were disgusting!

They were stained with mud and grass from the school field.

They were marked with drips of tomato sauce and custard where Trevor had been careless at lunchtime; they were spattered with blue paint from his last art lesson.

There was no doubt about it - Trevor's trousers were truly disgusting!

There was a patch on one knee, slightly darker than the surrounding material, from when Trevor had fallen in the school playground. One back pocket was hanging off from when he had caught it on the bottom of the school fence. Trevor had been trying to scramble underneath to get his football back.

'I don't know how you get them into such a state!' complained his mother, holding up Trevor's trousers at arms length. 'This is the third pair of trousers you've ruined since the beginning of term!'

'It just sort of . . . happens,' explained Trevor, feebly. 'I don't mean to make a mess of them - it just sort of happens.'

'Well, it's not good enough,' said Trevor's mum, dropping the offending trousers into a black plastic bag. 'I'm not made of money, you know. Trousers don't grow on trees!'

A thin smile crept across Trevor's face as an image of a tree hung with trousers floated into his mind.

'It's not funny, Trevor!' snapped Mum, angrily. You've got to make more effort to look after your clothes. You can't go to school looking like an old tramp. What will people think?'

'I'm sorry, Mum,' said Trevor, sincerely. 'I'll be more careful with the next pair. I promise.'

'Well, as it happens,' began Trevor's mum, reaching for her shopping bag, 'I've bought you some new trousers from the supermarket, only because they were on offer, mind you!'

Trevor's mum opened the bag and pulled out a pair of dark grey school trousers with a reduced price ticket stuck on the bottom.

'What do you think?'

'Lovely!' said Trevor, trying his best to sound enthusiastic. In truth, they looked exactly the same as all the other grey school trousers Trevor had ruined. 'Thanks Mum, they're really lovely!'

'Yes, well you make sure you look after them,' said Trevor's mum, handing them over. 'You'll get no more trousers until next term.'

Five minutes later, Trevor was in his bedroom trying on his new trousers. They were a little bit loose around the waist and rather long in the leg.

Still, he could wear a belt and he was
growing so quickly that they would probably
fit him perfectly in a few weeks time – if
they lasted that long!

Chapter 2
Off to School

The following morning was wet.

Trevor set off for school determined to return home later that day in pristine condition.

'I won't be playing football,' he thought, as he closed the front gate, 'because it's raining. Mum's packed some paper towels in my lunchbox so that I don't dribble on my trousers at dinner time – and the next art lesson isn't until Friday. Brilliant! There should be no problem!'

Trevor stood to one side as Mr Liptrot, his next door neighbour, advanced along the pavement with his dog, Buster. Buster was a huge, hairy brown spaniel who had a habit of jumping up at anyone he recognised.

'Can't have that,' thought Trevor, as he flattened himself against the wall. 'I don't want dirty paw marks and dog hairs on my new trousers.'

'Good morning, Trevor,' said Mr Liptrot, as he dragged Buster past. 'You're looking very smart today.'

'New trousers,' replied Trevor, keeping one eye on the panting dog. 'My mum said I've got to look after them.'

A little further along the road, Trevor spotted his best friend, Joe Knott, on the pavement opposite. He was just about to cross over when a double-decker bus turned the corner and picked up speed. Trevor stared down in horror at the great, dirty puddle in the road – but it was too late! The bus ploughed through sending a torrent of water into the air. Trevor let out a yell and leapt backwards as a wave of filthy water soaked him from head to foot.

He stood there, dripping wet, shaking his fist after the bus as it disappeared along the road.

'Did you see that!' stormed Trevor, as he joined his friend on the other side of the road. 'I'm sure that bus driver did it deliberately!'

'Don't let it worry you,' said Joe, reassuringly. 'A little bit of water never hurt anyone.'

'But I've got some new trousers,' explained Trevor, shaking a leg. 'I promised not to get them messy.'

'Too late now,' said Joe. 'Never mind, I'm sure they'll dry out once you get to school.'

The boys continued on their way, Trevor feeling damp and uncomfortable.

He had been out of the house for less than ten minutes and his trousers were soaked through.

As they entered the school playground, some girls from Trevor's class started giggling and pointing towards them.

'New trousers?' shouted Samantha Smith. They look a bit big!'

'I'll grow into them,' snapped Trevor, and he walked off in the opposite direction.

Samantha Smith had a soft spot for Trevor. Trevor couldn't stand her or her silly friends.

The whistle sounded for the start of the school day and the children lined up ready to enter the building. As they were waiting to go in, Trevor felt someone poke him in the back and he turned around to see Sidney Pratt smirking at him.

Sidney Pratt was Trevor's worst enemy. He was a sly, cunning boy who delighted in getting others into trouble.

He was as thin as a stick and he wore brown rimmed glasses that seemed to make his eyes bulge. He was so unpopular that everyone referred to him as *Sneaky Sid*.

'New trousers?' hissed Sneaky Sid. 'They're too big for you! You look ridiculous! Couldn't your mother afford to get you a pair that fitted properly?'

'Why don't you mind your own business?' retorted Trevor. 'At least I don't look like a stick insect!'

An angry voice boomed across the playground.

'Will you turn around and face the front, Trevor!' It was Mrs Blunt, the teacher on duty. 'I'm surprised at you, talking in the line! You really should know better!'

Sneaky Sid sniggered in delight.

Trevor scowled at him and turned to face the front, still feeling damp and irritable.

Chapter 3
The Ruby Ring

Trevor got through the rest of the school day without any further mishaps.

His trousers had dried out by lunchtime and, although they were slightly stained from his encounter with the double-decker bus, there was a good chance that his mother would not notice.

It was as Trevor was walking home after football practice that the strangest thing happened.

He was just feeling pleased with himself, having played well and scored two goals, when he spotted Sneaky Sid peddling like mad towards him on a bike that looked at least two sizes too small. Sneaky Sid kept glancing back behind him, as if he was being followed.

The next moment, two scruffy figures appeared from around a corner, pointed at Sneaky Sid and then charged after him. Trevor didn't recognise them. They looked older and they appeared to be very angry.

Sneaky Sid was getting closer and closer. He was riding on the pavement and he seemed completely unaware that Trevor was in his way.

At the last minute, Trevor let out a yell and Sneaky Sid slammed on his brakes. There was a scream of tyres, the bike skidded and slid across the wet pavement and Sneaky Sid flew through the air and landed with a thump at Trevor's feet.

The two scruffy youths pointed and raced forward. Sid staggered to his feet, shook himself and looked around in panic. He grabbed hold of Trevor's arm and pressed something into the palm of his hand.

'Look after this!' he gasped. 'Don't ask any questions! I'll get it back tomorrow!'

And then he was gone, charging away down the road for all he was worth, leaving his bike lying in a mangled heap in the gutter.

Trevor just stood there with his eyes wide and his mouth open, the mystery object clutched firmly in his hand.

The two youths barged past him in their hurry to get after Sneaky Sid. They nearly knocked him off his feet. It was only when they had disappeared from sight that Trevor opened his fist ever so slowly to reveal a beautiful ruby ring nestling in the palm of his hand.

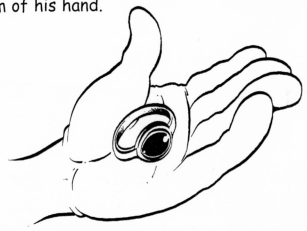

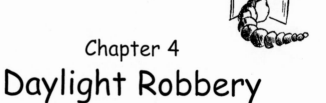

Chapter 4
Daylight Robbery

'Not too bad,' said Trevor's mum, slowly.

She had made him stand in the middle of the kitchen and she was carefully inspecting his new trousers.

'A few spots and marks but generally not too bad.'

'The marks aren't my fault,' explained Trevor. 'I got drenched on my way to school this morning by a passing double-decker bus.'

'Excuses, excuses . . . ' muttered Trevor's dad. He was sitting at the kitchen table reading his evening newspaper. 'You shouldn't make excuses, Trevor!'

'I suggest you go upstairs and get changed,' continued Mum. 'And get a move on! Your dinner will be on the table in five minutes!'

Trevor was just about to turn and leave the kitchen when he caught sight of the front page of the evening paper. He edged forward and stared over his dad's shoulder. A bold headline proclaimed: *Daylight Robbery!* Beneath the headline was a picture of the famous pop star Priscilla Peckham, who was being comforted by her rich husband Roland.

'Would you believe it!' said Trevor's dad, jabbing a finger towards the picture. 'Robbed in broad daylight when she came to open the new shopping centre. I don't know what this country's coming to!'

Trevor felt uneasy. He leaned further forward and read the report:

'Pop queen Priscilla Peckham is said to be in a state of shock having been robbed of her priceless ruby ring whilst opening The Gifford Centre earlier today. Priscilla, who was on a platform specially built for the occasion, was just about to cut the red ribbon when two youths wearing hooded tops leapt onto the staging and pulled the ring from her left hand. The robbers escaped into the crowd and were later seen running from the centre.

Priscilla's footballing husband, Roland was quoted as saying: "She's very upset. It was 'er favourite ring. I'll 'av to buy 'er another one now!"

Trevor stared at the picture and a cold shiver ran down his spine.

'Priceless ruby ring . . . ' he repeated, and ever so slowly he lowered his hand and placed it on his back pocket where, for safe keeping, he had put the ruby ring Sneaky Sid had pressed into his palm.

Upstairs, in his bedroom, Trevor stared at the sparkling ruby ring and he remembered the look of fear on Sneaky Sid's face.

He knew he should contact the police or, at the very least, tell his mum and dad about the ring. But what if he was wrong? What if it wasn't Priscilla Peckham's priceless ruby ring?

No, he would wait.

He would take the ring into school the next day and he would wait for Sneaky Sid to approach him. He would make sure of his facts and then he would hand the ring over to his teacher, Mrs Blunt.

Yes, Trevor liked that plan. He returned the ring carefully to the back pocket of his new trousers and he smiled to himself in satisfaction as he thought of the fun he was going to have with Sneaky Sid.

Chapter 5
The Ambush

It was nine o'clock at night and Sneaky Sid
was on his way home from the Fish and Chip
shop. He stuffed the last few soggy chips
into his mouth, threw the wrapping paper
onto the floor and wiped his greasy hands
on his jumper. He was totally unaware of the
ambush that awaited him around the next
corner.

Wayne Stubbs and Kevin Clegg were
lurking in the shadows between two
buildings, their hooded tops pulled high
around their heads.

'He's on his way,' whispered Wayne, peeping out from behind the wall. 'We can get him when he comes around the corner.'

Sneaky Sid did not stand a chance. He sauntered around the corner, his hands deep in his pockets and he did not know what had hit him.

Wayne and Kevin waited until he had just gone past and then they jumped out and dragged him backwards into the alleyway between the two tall buildings. Sneaky Sid tried to yell for help but Wayne placed a large, grubby hand over his mouth.

The two sneering thieves pinned Sid against the wall.

'So – you thought you'd try and trick us, did you?' snarled Wayne. 'Well, you picked the wrong ones, that's for sure!'

'Yes, that's for sure!' repeated Kevin, nodding his head up and down. Kevin wasn't too bright.

'We had a deal,' continued Wayne.

'When we slipped you the ring, you were supposed to get as far away from the shopping centre as you could on your bike and then you were to give the ring back to us. Remember? What happened to our deal?'

Sneaky Sid looked terrified. His eyes were wide and he was shaking with fear.

'Well, what have you got to say for yourself?' barked Wayne.

'He can't say anything,' pointed out Kevin. 'You've got your hand over his mouth!'

'I know that, bonehead!' snapped Wayne, lowering his hand. 'I don't need you to tell me!'

'I was going to give it back – honest!' stammered Sneaky Sid. 'But I haven't got it anymore!'

Wayne's face turned purple with rage. He looked like a boiled beetroot.

'Haven't got it!' he stormed. 'What do you mean you haven't got it?'

'Yes, what do you mean you haven't got it?' added Kevin, determined to join in.

'Where is it?'

'I – I – passed it on to someone,' mumbled Sid, fiddling with his glasses. 'A boy in my class at school. His name's Trevor.'

Wayne looked as if he was about to explode. 'You just handed it over to some idiot called Trevor?' he fumed. 'Do you know how much that ring is worth?'

'It's priceless,' said Kevin, helpfully. 'I read about it in the paper.'

Wayne glared at him as Sneaky Sid shook even more.

'I'll get it back from him,' stammered Sid. 'I'll see him at school tomorrow and I'll get it back from him. I promise.'

'You'd better,' said Wayne, relaxing his grip, 'because if you don't . . . '

He left the threat unfinished but Sneaky Sid was in no doubt what would happen to him if he failed to recover the ruby ring.

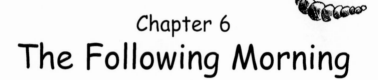

Chapter 6
The Following Morning

The following morning Trevor set off for
school bright and early.

He had placed the ruby ring in a
brown envelope for safe keeping and he had
stuffed the brown envelope carefully into
the back pocket of his new trousers.

It was wet again and Trevor stood
well back from the kerb as he waited to
cross the road to join his friend Joe. Sure
enough, the double-decker bus appeared
from around the corner and ploughed

through the puddle, sending a spray of dirty water up into the air and over the pavement.

'Missed me!' muttered Trevor but he was sure he saw the driver smirk as he drove past.

Trevor couldn't wait to tell Joe about the ruby ring. He glanced around to make sure that nobody was looking and then he produced the envelope from his back pocket and took out the ring.

Joe's eyes opened wide in disbelief as the priceless gem sparkled before him. He listened in amazement as Trevor told him how he came to have the ring.

Joe had heard about the robbery in the shopping centre and he had seen an interview with the sobbing Priscilla Peckham on the evening news.

'You've got to give it back,' he urged. 'There's a full scale search on for that ring – and for the thieves who snatched it!'

'Of course I'll give it back,' explained Trevor, returning the ring to the envelope. 'I'm going to hand it over to Mrs Blunt – but I might just have a bit of fun first. Sneaky Sid is in this up to his scrawny little neck and I want to make sure he's caught.'

'It'll end in disaster,' said Joe, shaking his head. 'I just know it will end in disaster!'

There was no sign of Sneaky Sid in the school playground. Trevor was surprised. He had expected Sid to be waiting for him, ready to demand back the ring but he was nowhere to be seen. Just as the whistle blew, Joe pointed over towards the school gate.

'He's there, talking to those two scruffy youths. They look a bit suspicious to me.'

Trevor recognised them immediately. They were the same two scruffy youths who had been chasing Sid the previous evening. One of them pushed Sid into the yard and wagged a finger at him, threateningly.

Trevor made sure he was behind Sid in the line, this time.

As they were waiting for their turn to go into school, Sneaky Sid turned around and said: 'O.K., where is it, Trevor?'

'I don't know what you're talking about,' replied Trevor, innocently.

'The ring!' hissed Sneaky Sid, his face turning red. 'The ruby ring! It belongs to my mother and I want it back!'

'Belongs to your mother,' repeated Trevor, slowly, and then he snapped, 'You're lying! Why would you press your mum's ring into my hand and then run off?'

'Because . . . because . . . because someone was trying to steal it from me,' replied Sid, unconvincingly. 'Now where is it?'

'Don't you worry, it's quite safe,' said Trevor, patting his back pocket. 'And I promise I'll make sure it gets back to its rightful owner.'

Sneaky Sid was about to say something threatening when Mrs Blunt's angry voice barked out his name.

'Sidney Pratt! Is that the back of your head I can see? Turn and face the front at once!'

'I'll see you later,' growled Sneaky Sid, and he shuffled forward in irritation as the children began to move into school.

Chapter 7
The Deserted Room

Later that morning, Trevor's class gathered in the school hall for their weekly P.E. lesson.

Once he was changed into his shorts and t-shirt, Trevor made a huge show of folding his trousers neatly and placing them on his chair.

Sneaky Sid's face looked as black as thunder. He scowled at Trevor and screwed up his eyes in hate.

After the warm up, Mrs Blunt told the children that she was going to divide them up for team games. It was then that she realised she had left her whistle in the classroom.

'I need a volunteer to go back to class and fetch my whistle,' said Mrs Blunt, looking round. 'Who can I trust to do that important job?'

Trevor was about to step forward when Sneaky Sid's hand shot into the air. He waved it about frantically to catch Mrs Blunt's attention.

'I'll go, Miss,' he said, doing his best to sound helpful. 'You can trust me to fetch your whistle.'

The other children looked amazed. Sneaky Sid never offered to help anyone and he particularly hated P.E. He usually did his best to spoil the lesson.

Trevor knew exactly why Sid wanted to go back into the classroom but there was nothing he could do about it. He glanced across at Joe and shrugged his shoulders.

Mrs Blunt looked most surprised but, keen to encourage him, she called Sneaky Sid forward.

'It's in the top drawer of my desk,' she informed him, handing over the classroom key. 'Be as quick as you can and be sure to lock the classroom door when you leave.'

Sneaky Sid slid out of the school hall, turning to give Trevor a sly grin as Mrs Blunt began to split the class into teams. He couldn't believe his luck. He would be all alone in the classroom with Trevor's trousers. No one could stop him from claiming back the ruby ring.

A couple of minutes later, Sneaky Sid turned the key in the lock and entered the deserted classroom.

It felt strange. It was so quiet. For some reason, Sid felt quite nervous but he was determined to recover the ruby ring.

'I'd better get the whistle first,' Sneaky Sid muttered to himself, and his voice seemed to echo around the empty room.

He crossed to the teacher's desk and pulled open the top drawer. There was the whistle, right in the corner.

Sid grabbed the whistle and helped himself to one of Mrs Blunt's boiled sweets that she always kept hidden in her drawer.

'She won't miss one,' he convinced himself, and he slipped the sweet into his mouth and the whistle into the pocket of his P.E. shorts.

He was just about to close the drawer when he caught sight of the scissors, Mrs Blunt's extra large, extra sharp classroom scissors.

A thin, cruel grin spread across Sneaky Sid's face as he grabbed the scissors, closed the drawer and headed for Trevor's trousers.

'Try to trick me, would he?' muttered Sid, menacingly. 'I'll teach him a lesson!'

Sid grabbed Trevor's trousers from the chair and made a deep cut into one leg. It was so satisfying! He withdrew the scissors and then cut again. He couldn't stop.

The right leg of Trevor's new trousers was cut into ribbons! He was just about to start on the left leg when the classroom door opened suddenly and Mr Brush, the school caretaker, stepped inside clutching a black plastic sack.

Sid dropped the scissors in shock and kicked them under the nearest table so that the caretaker couldn't see them.

'Now then, lad,' began Mr Brush, surprised to find anyone in the classroom, 'what are you up to?'

'Up to?' repeated Sneaky Sid, doing his best to sound innocent. 'I'm not up to anything. I'm just getting Mrs Blunt's whistle for her.'

Mr Brush stared at the shredded trousers that Sid still clutched in his hands. 'They're in a bit of a state,' he said. 'How did they get like that?'

'Oh, they're only my old trousers,' lied Sid. 'I was just going to get rid of them.'

'Drop 'em in the bin, then,' said Mr Brush, nodding towards the classroom waste paper basket. 'They're no use to you like that, are they?'

Sneaky Sid gave a gulp.

The ring was still in the back pocket. Why hadn't he removed it before he had destroyed the trousers?

'Go on then, lad!' prompted Mr Brush, and he picked up the waste paper basket and held it out towards Sid.

Sneaky Sid had no choice. He dropped Trevor's trousers into the bin and stared with wide, bulging eyes at the caretaker.

'Off you go, then,' said Mr Brush,
emptying the bin into his black plastic sack.
'Don't worry about the door – I'll lock it
when I've finished.'

Outside in the corridor, Sneaky Sid slid down the wall and sat with his head in his hands. How was he going to explain to Wayne and Kevin that he had thrown Priscilla Peckham's priceless ruby ring into the classroom rubbish bin?

Chapter 8
The Bin Wagon

Sneaky Sid knew he had to act quickly. All was not lost – the ring was still there in the back pocket of Trevor's trousers.

If he could just get the trousers back from Mr Brush's black sack . . .

And then it came to him! 'Of course!' he said out loud. 'Old Brush will empty the sack into the big bin at the back of school. All I've got to do is follow him, wait for my chance . . . and the ring will be mine!'

Feeling much happier now that he had a plan, Sneaky Sid sprang to his feet and waited around the nearest corner for Mr Brush to leave the classroom.

Back in the hall, Mrs Blunt was angry and impatient.

'Where is that boy? He's been ten minutes already! I knew I shouldn't have trusted him to fetch my whistle!'

Trevor took his chance. 'Shall I go and look for him, Miss?' he said, stepping forward. 'Perhaps Joe could come with me?'

'Go on, then,' agreed Mrs Blunt. 'But be quick about it! The lesson will be over if you don't get a move on!'

The two boys left the hall and headed for the classroom.

'He's up to no good,' said Trevor, quickening his pace. 'I just know he's up to no good!'

They turned the corner into the main corridor to be met by the strangest sight. Sidney Pratt was creeping along the corridor on tip-toe. Ahead of him was Mr Brush, the school caretaker, whistling cheerfully as he went about his business.

Sneaky Sid looked like a sly fox stalking his prey.

'What do you make of that?' whispered Joe. 'What's he doing?'

'I don't know,' replied Trevor, keeping his voice low, 'but I think we should find out. Come on!'

Sneaky Sid had no idea he was being followed. His eyes were firmly fixed on the caretaker. Joe and Trevor edged forward until they were level with the classroom window.

Trevor wasn't sure why he did it, but he glanced through the window into the empty classroom.

He knew something was wrong immediately. He wasn't sure what – but he could sense that something was wrong. And then he looked at his chair and let out a low gasp. His trousers were missing. They were not on the chair where he had left them. His mum would go mad!

'He's stolen my pants!' whispered Trevor, angrily. 'That little sneak has stolen my new trousers!'

'He can't have done,' said Joe. 'He's not got them with him, has he?'

'My trousers are not where I left them,' snapped Trevor, 'and we both know that little sneak went back into class.'

'Wait a minute,' said Joe, slowly raising a finger and pointing past Sid towards the school caretaker. 'What's that?'

He had spotted Mr Brush's black sack.

Trevor strained his eyes to see and then he let out a horrified gasp. One torn and tattered trouser leg was trailing out from the top of the sack.

'My trousers!' hissed Trevor, his lip quivering with rage. 'My new trousers are in shreds! He's going to throw them in the bin!'

'Keep calm!' urged Joe, scared that they would attract attention. 'This is our chance to trap Sneaky Sid. We can catch him red handed!'

The two boys crept along the corridor behind Sneaky Sid who in turn was following the school caretaker. Mr Brush left the building by a side door and Sid followed a few seconds later.

Trevor and Joe counted to ten before opening the door cautiously and peeping out. The coast was clear. They edged around the building until they could see the big bins at the back of the school. At first, there was no sign of Sneaky Sid and then Joe noticed him crouched behind a bush, watching the caretaker's every move.

Mr Brush lifted the sack over the edge of the huge round bin and shook it forcefully. When he withdrew the sack, it was empty. The caretaker walked off around the back of the school, whistling to himself cheerfully.

Sneaky Sid waited until the caretaker was out of sight and then stepped from his hiding place in the bush.

'Now we'll have him!' said Trevor, in anticipation. 'Just wait until he moves towards the bin!'

Sneaky Sid was just about to advance when there was a roar from the direction of the school gates. He was so startled that he ducked back down behind the bush.

Trevor and Joe glanced towards the gates and their mouths dropped open in horror. A huge bin wagon was advancing up the driveway. There was no stopping it! It was bin day! The men were coming to empty the big bins and take the rubbish to the town tip!

Chapter 9
The Town Tip

The bin wagon screeched to a halt and the crew jumped out of the cab and loaded the big waste bin onto the back platform.

It was empty within seconds and the men had wheeled it back into position before Sneaky Sid had fully realised what was happening. The men got back into the cab and the wagon began to drive off.

It was then that Sneaky Sid leapt into life. He raced from his hiding place behind the bush and jumped onto the back platform of the bin wagon.

Trevor and Joe stumbled out onto the drive and watched in dismay as the wagon disappeared up the drive. Sneaky Sid saw them at once and he waved and blew them each a kiss.

The wagon slowed as it passed through the school gates and two more figures jumped onto the back platform.

Trevor recognised the figures at once. Wayne and Kevin had been watching and waiting. They had no intention of allowing Sneaky Sid to ride away with the ruby ring.

'We can't just let them escape,' gasped Trevor. 'They're going to fish my trousers out of the bin wagon!'

'I'm pretty sure this is their last stop,' said Joe. 'The wagon will be heading straight for the town tip.'

The two boys looked at each other for a matter of seconds and then nodded.

'Come on!' urged Trevor. 'We can cut across the school field and get to the tip before them!'

Back in the school hall, Mrs Blunt was feeling very stressed. 'I don't believe it!' she sighed, clasping a hand to her forehead. 'That's three children I've lost! Vanished into thin air! There'll be no one left in the class soon!'

'Shall I go and look for them?' suggested Emma Parkin.

'No! No!' screamed the teacher. 'No one else is to leave the hall!'

Trevor and Joe raced across the school field and out of the back gate. They rushed past a couple of old ladies who were out for their morning walk.

'That's two more escaped,' commented one of the old ladies. 'What do you think they do to them in there?'

The two boys cut through a back alleyway and over some rough ground and after a few minutes they arrived outside the entrance to the town tip. Trevor looked through the huge metal gates and was astonished to see the mountains of rubbish.

'It's massive,' he panted. He was gasping to get his breath back. 'I've never been here before!'

Inside the gates a rough track led to the first huge pile of rubbish, which was stacked high, waiting to be sorted. A bin wagon was just pulling away having tipped its load.

Trevor had not seen anything like it. A mountain of black bags were piled high, kitchen waste leaking out and sliding down the tip, broken chairs, an old spring mattress ripped and torn – every type of rubbish imaginable.

The smell was awful. Joe screwed up his nose in disgust.

Seagulls circled overhead and swooped every so often to pick up pieces of stale bread or bits of someone's left-over dinner.

A huge crane with a bucket like a set of jaws was dumping more rubbish onto the top of the tip. It looked like a great extinct dinosaur, its neck swinging backwards and forwards, its mouth opening and closing.

The crane stopped suddenly and the operator jumped down from the cab and went for his tea break.

'What do we do now?' asked Trevor, scratching his head.

He had no sooner spoken than another bin wagon appeared from around the corner and headed for the great gates. The two boys ducked down and watched as the wagon entered the site and drove towards the mountain of rubbish. This was the one they had been waiting for!

Sneaky Sid and the two youths were still clinging on to the back of the wagon.

Chapter 10
Caught in the Act

Sneaky Sid and his two scruffy friends leapt off the bin wagon as it came to a halt and darted behind the monster crane. The bin wagon reversed up to the tip and the back of the wagon began to tilt so that it could empty its rubbish.

'My trousers are in there!' groaned Trevor, as he watched the rubbish start to slide out. 'My new trousers are going to end up on the town tip!'

'Yes, it's bad luck,' agreed Joe. 'Let's watch and see what happens next!'

The rubbish tumbled out from the back of the wagon, sending the seagulls swirling in excitement. The back of the wagon was lowered into position and the driver and his crew set off for their next collection.

Sneaky Sid and his friends were onto the tip within seconds. They scrambled across the black bags trying to get to the freshly dumped rubbish.

They stumbled and slid in their haste to find Trevor's trousers. They didn't notice the driver arrive back at his crane and they didn't hear the growl of the engine as the great monster roared into life.

Trevor and Joe stood and watched with their mouths open. They knew what was going to happen next. Sure enough, the jaws of the crane grasped a pile of filthy, dripping rubbish and swung it high into the air.

There was a shout from Sneaky Sid as he reached the top of the tip.

'I've got them! I've got them!' he yelled, and he held up Trevor's torn and tattered trousers for all to see.

The jaws of the monster crane opened and the rubbish cascaded down, covering Sneaky Sid from head to foot.

Wayne and Kevin screamed in fright as the crane swooped again. They pushed each other and shoved and stumbled in their haste to escape. Wayne took a flying leap and crashed to the ground, where he rolled around in pain and clutched at his ankle.

Kevin got his foot caught in the old spring mattress and he looked up in horror as the jaws of the crane opened again and more rubbish poured out.

Sneaky Sid just stood there, at the top of the tip, completely covered in dirty, smelly rubbish.

His clothes were covered with clogged custard and he had spaghetti dripping from his head.

Trevor and Joe had moved into the yard and they were doubled up with laughter. They couldn't stop! The tears were streaming down Trevor's face!

There was a sudden shout as the site manager appeared. At the same time, the crane driver had spotted the intruders and turned off his engine.

'What on earth is going on?' stormed the site manager. 'Into my office – all of you! We'll see what the police have to say about this!'

'I can't move . . . ' came a feeble, whimpering voice. It was Kevin from half way up the tip. 'I've got my foot stuck in a mattress . . !'

Chapter 11
The Reward

'You didn't honestly think I'd leave the ring in the back pocket of my trousers, did you?' said Trevor, with a sly smile.

They were gathered together in the site manager's office, waiting for the police to arrive.

Joe was holding his nose. Sneaky Sid smelt awful. He still had some stale spaghetti tangled in his hair and stuck to his glasses.

'I gave the ring to Mrs Blunt first thing this morning,' continued Trevor. 'It was in an envelope with a note explaining exactly how I got it. I know she passed it straight on to the Headteacher.'

Wayne and Kevin snarled and glared at Sneaky Sid.

'But . . . but . . . I don't understand . . .' stammered Sneaky Sid, looking shocked. He still had hold of Trevor's tattered trousers.

'Why did you follow me to the tip?'

'There was no way I was going to let you escape,' explained Trevor. 'I knew you'd find my trousers and discover the pocket was empty. I wanted to make sure you got what you deserved!'

At that moment, the door to the office opened and a large policeman stepped inside. He was clutching hold of the note Trevor had written about the ruby ring.

'Oh, he'll get what he deserves, all right,' said the policeman, staring directly at Sneaky Sid, 'and so will these other two rascals! Come on, there's a car outside waiting to take you to the police station!'

It was two days later that the package arrived.

News about the recovery of Priscilla Peckham's priceless ruby ring had been splashed all over the newspapers. It had even been reported on the television news.

There were pictures of a delighted Priscilla proudly displaying her ring, her smiling husband in the background, happy that he did not have to buy her a replacement.

When Trevor's mum opened the door, she was astonished to see a posh black Cadillac parked in the road at the front of the house.

A tall man in a grey uniform was holding up a package wrapped in silver paper and decorated with a large red ribbon.

'It's for your son, Trevor,' he explained. 'Just a little something from Miss Peckham to say thank you for returning her ring.'

The man turned and walked off down the path without saying another word. He got into the Cadillac and drove away at speed.

'Trevor!' shouted Mum from the bottom of the stairs. 'Trevor! Get down here at once! Priscilla Peckham's sent you a reward! How exciting is that? Come and see what it is!'

Trevor's bedroom door flew open and he leapt down the stairs three at a time.

He grabbed the package and ripped off the wrapping paper.

He threw the lid to one side and pulled out . . .

. . . a pair of trousers!

Priscilla Peckham had sent him a pair of grey school trousers!

'Oh, well,' sighed Mum, as Trevor held up the trousers in disbelief, 'I suppose it's the thought that counts!'

THE END